The Adventures of Lily Sutton#3

Hidden Covers

Book Three

Other Books by Linda Scott Enakevwe

More Than It Seems – The Jimmy Jurrell High School E Z Peezy Series – eBook

More Than It Seems – The Jimmy Jurrell High School E Z Peezy Series – Trade Paperback

A Handed Down Legacy – A Lesson From Beyond – eBook

A Handed Down Legacy – A Lesson From Beyond – (Library Distribution) Trade Paperback

   The Ad. Of Lily Sutton books 1-3 are for ages 10 and older

Mirrors – The Adventures of Lily Sutton – Book #1 – eBook

Mirrors – The Adventures of Lily Sutton – Book #1 – (Library Distribution) Trade Paperback

One Drunk in the Family Is Enough – The Adventures of Lily Sutton - Book #2 - Trade Paperback

The Adventures of Lily Sutton – Hidden Covers – Book #3 – eBook

The Adventures of Lily Sutton – Hidden Covers – Book #3 – Trade Paperback (Ages 16+ years old)

   The Ad. Of Lily Sutton books 4-9 are for ages 16 and older

The Adventures of Lily Sutton – Choices – Book #4 – Trade Paperback

The Adventures of Lily Sutton – Lily's Choices – Book #4 – Trade (Library Dist.)

The Adventures of Lily Sutton #8 – A Woman's Intuition - Trade Paperback

School Is More Than It Seems (Library Distribution) – Trade Paperback

Religious Title

Forgiveness Is Not For the Birds –

Forgiveness is For the Children of God

See more of the series: The Adventures of Lily Sutton, a nine book series.

The Adventures of Lily Sutton #5 Love Postponed (for 16+year olds)

The Adventures of Lily's Sutton #6 Lily's Jimmy (for 16+year olds)

The Adventures of Lily Sutton #7 Lily's Forgotten Dreams (for 16+year olds)

The Adventures of Lily Sutton #9 Lily's Chances (for 16+year olds)

The Adventures of Lily Sutton #3

Hidden Covers

By

LINDA SCOTT ENAKEVWE

(Enak ev we)

The Enakevwe who loves God

Circle of Friends Publishing Company – Houston, Texas

Copyright Page

The Adventures of Lily Sutton
Hidden Covers
Book Three

Circle of Friends Publishing Company
A division of Jimmy Jurrell Company
P. O. Box 710352
Houston, TX 77271-0352

To my children and grandchildren

for their continued love and support

The Adventures of Lily Sutton

Hidden Covers – Book Three

It was early June in Morrows, Louisiana, a small town about twenty miles south of Landry, Louisiana. Lily Sutton and her parents had moved back to Morrows weeks earlier. Her parents had spent almost forty years in Morrows, but work and opportunity had taken them to Landry for two years. That little spurt of growth in Landry had dried up to the same lack of opportunity that Morrows had always been known to have. Lucky for them, their house was vacant again after one of Lily's sisters packed her bags and took her four kids to live in Galveston, Texas, totally fed up with living in Morrows.

Out of the blue, Lily's sister, who had lived there for three years, decided she had had enough of her husband William and she wanted a change.

After Alice Sutton asked her older daughter questions and didn't get any answers, she packed her bags, Lily's bags, and her husband's bags and moved from Landry back into her house in Morrows. With very little work in Morrows, the common ingredient that kept everybody going was gossip. It was always easier for someone to laugh at someone else's problems on the outside than to take a look at their own problems on the inside.

Lily and her mother did not have to wait long for a laugh at someone else's problems as people put on their best outfits to send off another dearly departed soul whose roots had been deeply embedded in Morrows, Louisiana.

The sun set slowly as half the town of around one-hundred people began to fill Plymouth Rock Baptist Church for a wake. Regardless of who the deceased was, everyone came out to pay his last respects and, of course, talk about each other. Very few people knew the deceased, but everyone knew her mother, Bessie, and wanted to comfort Bessie.

The deceased was Darla Bennard, a woman born in Morrows, Louisiana who had lived in Chicago for fifteen years. The obituary identified her as thirty-five years old and as having had two children. It was hard to tell how old she was by looking at her face in the casket. She was dark-complexioned and had a round, ordinary face with thin pancake-shaped lips and puffy cheeks. She had huge eye-sockets and a receding hairline that someone had tried to cover with a forced bang made with hair from the top of her head. A tall, thin Black woman named Christy, who was wearing a tailored white pantsuit, kept going to the casket fixing the hair of the deceased. Christy lived in Chicago and had been a good friend to Darla. It was said that she had traveled to Morrows to sing at Darla's funeral.

As darkness settled on the little town, the deacons of the church organized the prayer service. People took their seats, and Mrs. Martha Williams, the musician, played the piano for the choir to sing. Lily Sutton, stood and led the choir in a prayer service hymn.

After the choir and the congregation finished singing a few songs, Christy walked into the choir. The audience stared and smiled at Christy's beauty. She had heavily made-up, striking facial features and stood over six feet tall in average-heeled boots. She went to the piano and leaned down to talk to Mrs. Martha. Moments later, Mrs. Martha and a few deacons turned the piano around so that the back of the piano and whomever was playing it could face the audience.

Christy sat down at the piano, smiling at the choir and the audience as she rearranged her hair with her fingers.

"You don't need to sing on this number. I'll be singing solo," Christy said to the choir in a heavy, raspy voice.

She turned and smiled at the audience. Everyone in the church gazed in quiet anticipation. They were not accustomed to great singing or great piano playing coming out of the choir at that little church. They were longing for a treat.

"I want to make sure the audience can see my eyes when I sing," Christy explained. "Is this okay, honey?"

Lily Sutton gave Christy a puzzled look but nodded briefly and quickly. Alice turned around and looked at the other choir members, trying to see if they had heard what she had heard. Everyone's face was transfixed on Christy. Each was caught up in the glamour of Christy's behavior.

Christy struck a chord on the piano keys that rewarded the complete attention she had received from the entire congregation. She played the piano and fluttered her eye lashes. The audience seemed thrilled. That piano had never been played as well. Everyone for miles around Morrows had become accustomed to Mrs. Martha as a piano player. Only a few guest singers who visited the little church ever allowed Mrs. Martha to accompany them after she played the first chord of their intended song. Many guest singers preferred to sing acappella.

Christy sang "Precious Lord," and she blinked her eyes and flirted with the audience on every stanza. Most of the men in the audience grinned and applauded as though they were at a concert instead of a wake. The men seemed to have been taken with Christy's flash of glamour.

She knew she looked special. She had short, black hair with wide fluffy bangs that laid like a wig. She was adorned with long false eyelashes, ruby red lipstick, diamond earrings, and dark, heavily made-up eyes that resembled those of a cocker spaniel. She performed in the spotlight, and the audience lovingly absorbed it all.

Christy was the best dressed, most stylish-looking woman who had ever been in Morrows. The way the men whispered in the audience while she sang was as though they were taking bets at a horse track.

Lily sat beside her mother in the choir, and glanced repeatedly from Christy to the audience. The people in the audience grinned and some even tried to clap after the second song. Near the end of Christy's third song, Lily caught a glimpse of her ex-brother-in-law, William Green, sitting in the audience whispering in a huddle of men. Lily whispered, "Mama, look at that clown, William. He's out there foaming at the mouth like an old dog...probably about Christy."

"All of them will be standing in line fighting over who's gonna take her out. You know that's how they act every time a new woman comes to town. The women act the same way every time a new man or a new preacher comes here. You would think grown people wouldn't act like that, even here in the country. They make it seem like we ain't used to nothing," Lily's mother added.

When the wake service ended, most of the people stood outside in the moonlight and socialized with the family. Almost every man, married or single, lingered near Christy. She talked in a strange, little girl's voice while in the company of the men. As Christy toyed with the men, Lily kept staring at her with a look of utter bewilderment. Something about Christy was not right. Lily's suspicious nature worked overtime, but she decided not to mention anything to the other women. The women knew they were going to have a hard time getting their men away from Christy, so they gathered their children and left the church.

Of all of the men on the church grounds, Christy left the church with the town's fool, William Green. William walked around the church grounds with his chest stuck out like a proud peacock. He bragged to the deacons that the woman wanted him.

"All of you old men can go home with your fat wives, because the lady is going out with the king," William boasted. "I'm the top dog tonight. The woman is leaving with me."

Lily finally found her mother on the church grounds and whispered something in her ears that seemed to startle Alice at first but brought a belated smile to her face. "Mama, do you think we should tell William what we think about Christy, or do you think we should let him learn a good lesson?" Lily asked.

"Don't say anything. Ain't no way we can know the real truth about that anyway," Alice said. "It is going to take one of the men to find that out. Let William Green find out the best way he knows how, just like a fool should. Besides, you can't tell him anything anyway. Your sister couldn't do anything with him when she was with him, so let Christy teach him a thing or two."

"You are right, Mama. Besides, the whole town could use a good laugh, especially our family."

After the wake, William took Christy to the family home of the deceased, where she would spend the week-end. He waited for her to change clothes before they left for a popular nightclub. He stood in the yard and talked to some of the men who had gathered there to visit with the family. William immediately began to impersonate a gentleman in front of his friends as he ran around the car to open the door for Christy. William's cousin, Kenneth, walked over to William and tried to enlighten him on the rumor that had, somehow, started after the wake had ended.

"Will, come here, man. I got something to tell you."

"What you want, Ken? Don't ask me nothing about this woman, and don't tell me nothing about my ex, because I'm not taking her back, even if she asks."

"Man, I ain't telling you nothing about no ex. I heard she doesn't want you back anyway. I want to tell you what I know about Christy."

"Ken, you don't know nothing about Christy. You and all of these other clowns can't tell me nothing about this woman. She's from Chicago. Y'all don't know her, and she don't know y'all. Now, that's that."

"Man, my mama lives in Chicago, and she's here for the

funeral, too. Now, I know you ain't calling my mama a liar. And what I got to tell you comes straight from her. So, now...what's it gonna be?"

"It ain't 'gonna be nothing, Ken, cause your mama ain't told you nothing. And if she did, I don't want to hear it."

"All right, Will. Forget I even mentioned anything. I mean, I was trying to do you a favor. I'm not getting any joy out of this. Besides, here comes Christy now, so forget I even tried to say anything."

Ken, shaking his head, walked away from William before Christy reached them. William drove off with Christy, the both of them heading for the night club, laughing and waving to Ken. He had risked getting his feelings hurt by even trying to advise William. None of the other townspeople would have bothered to help William because he always managed to make people feel sorry they even tried to help him.

William had been cursed with the gift of gab, but he had a habit of gabbing the wrong things at the wrong time. At thirty-seven years old, with two divorces behind him, William had never learned when to shut up. Often called a tall, lanky loudmouth, William was always threatening people, trying to make them angry, knowing he wasn't going to fight anyone. He had been transferred from his job on the railroad several times for teasing co-workers. One co-worker lost his temper with William's teasing and attacked him with an iron tool. The man had to be pulled off William by other workers. The supervisor transferred William to truck driving all day because no one on the railroad site wanted to be around him anymore. William enjoyed bringing up his co-workers' personal problems in front of other people. He had a warped, mindless sense of humor that made people want to hurt him.

Women disliked William in the same manner in which men disliked him. When it came down to insulting people, William Green knew no gender. He went into an extremely crowded convenience store in Bunkie, Louisiana one day and began to tease the clerk, Maxine Murray. Maxine was about three hundred pounds and five-feet five inches tall. Her childhood weight problem had not diminished her beauty. People constantly told her that she had a pretty face.

William entered the store, looked at Maxine and said, "Ugh, too big...you are too big. I would let you talk to my brother, but you are too big. Why you do that to yourself, Maxine? You need to lose some weight. Now."

Maxine turned beet red in the face while trying to restrain

herself from leaving the counter after William. "Let me tell you one thing, William Green. Don't think I won't cuss you out with your stupid self just because these people are in here. I don't play that mess, and I would not have your ugly brother anyway." He burst out laughing and ran out of the store at the same time that Maxine picked up a can of soda and gestured to throw it at him.

William Green forgot about all those people he had teased when he was seen with Christy. When they arrived at the nightclub, he was grinning like a comedian after telling one of his own jokes.

Christy had been quiet during the ten-mile drive from Morrows to the small town of Bunkie, Louisiana. Morrows, with no traffic or street lights, looked light years behind Chicago's skyline and enterprise. Bunkie was slightly larger than Morrows as it was labeled a town and had night clubs, a police station, and a few traffic lights.

The Big Top Nightclub had become the main attraction for town's people in Bunkie at night and was crowded with the Morrows regulars most of the time. William walked in talking loudly and grinning, with Christy holding onto his arm. He wanted to impress people with the good-looking stranger. He was trying his best to change his life-long reputation of being an unwanted, joke-cracking fool, but everybody still thought of William Green as being irritating and insulting. Even the children of women he dated cracked his face with insults every time they saw him.

As William walked around the nightclub looking for a perfect table, he knew in his heart that no one in the club wanted him to sit with them. His cousin, Nathan, recognized him blundering in the dark club and called out to him. Nathan had long ago accepted the notion that

William was crazy and he decided to over-look most of the insulting things William said to people.

"Hey William. Y'all can join us over here," Nathan yelled.

"Thanks, Man. I can hardly see in here. What's going on?"

"Nothing, Man. You got all the attention tonight with this beautiful lady."

"You know it. Oh, yeah, Nathan, this here is Christy. Christy, this here is Nathan, my cousin, and his wife Betty."

"Pleased to meet you guys," Christy said.

"Same here, Christy," Nathan said staring at her in the dark club with squinted eyes.

Christy looked away from Nathan's stares and summoned

the waitress. She ordered a martini, but after the waitress expressed confusion, Christy changed it to a vodka straight with a twist of lime.

"I keep forgetting I'm in the country," Christy said with a sudden foreign accent. "I'm so used to Chicago and everything being right there for me."

"You can get everything you need right here, Baby," William added. "This here is the country all right, but we ain't lacking for nothing. We're always feeding a whole bunch of kin folks from the city right here in the country. Some of them beg every time they call home. They need this, and they need that...Speaking of needing...Hey, Honey, bring me a pint. You know what I drink," William yelled to the waitress.

"Man, you had better slow down on that fire water. You

know we ain't got no cabs here in the country either," Nathan quipped.

William laughed. "Man, that's something else we got on them city dudes. We can drink more than they can and pay for it, too. But, Nathan, you know I ain't never had no problems driving my ride, even when I'm full of my oil. So you don't need to bring that up to me in front of my lady here, unless it's a joke," William said, chuckling.

"Hey, Man, I thought I would say something lively since both of y'all seem to be a little uptight. But I see you're all right, and I will stop because I show don't want to get you started," Nathan confessed.

William and Christy sat drinking with Nathan and Betty. Christy laughed at every joke that William said. She ignored Nathan and Betty completely. She hung on William's every word, and with each drink that she downed, she snuggled closer and closer to him. Betty became rather restless after being left out of every conversation. She stood and asked Christy if she wanted to go to the ladies room with her. Christy quickly shouted "no," without looking at Betty.

William said, "Baby, you better go on 'cause we 'gonna be leaving soon, and it's a long ride home. Otherwise, your two bathroom choices will be the woods or a trip back to Miss Bessie's house. Somehow, I know you don't want me taking you back to Miss Bessie's house, tonight?"

Christy stood and said, "You got it, Baby, and I don't want to 'go' in the woods either. I don't want to see Bessie until the funeral tomorrow. I'm with you, lover...all the way."

Betty stood first, and Christy followed her to the ladies' room. She towered over Betty and every other woman in the club. The line outside the stalls in the ladies' room stopped Betty in her tracks and she started complaining about the odor.

"The least they can do is clean this filthy place," Betty told Christy. "God knows people spend enough money on liquor and that ragged jukebox for them to pay somebody to clean this bathroom."

"I guess they don't intend for you to linger," Christy said. "In some of the clubs in Chicago, people be doing it so heavily, the managers have to hire an attendant to monitor the goings on in the restroom."

"Oh yeah? Somebody gets paid for sitting in there, huh? But I guess it is worth something to sit in there and smell the place."

"It's not the smell that is the problem, Honey. It's the dope and the sex they are trying to stop. Anyway, it does not do much good because the customers put a few dollars in the woman's can and still do what they want to do, even with her in there."

"You're kidding. I have always been scared of the big cities. Here is fine, but it is the same old, same old. Maybe one day, Nathan and I can get away to some place nice. Right now, we don't go anywhere but work and here to this here club on the week-ends."

"Well...uh, what's your name again?" Christy asked.

"Betty."

"Well, Betty, I didn't think I had to go at first, but suddenly, I have waited all I can. I am going back to the table to wait, or, better yet, where is the men's room? I can go in there and be out in a second. A bathroom is a bathroom."

"Girl, you can't go in there. One of those men will go in on you for sure."

"I'm not worried about that," Christy said.

"But what will people think?"

"They can think whatever they want to think. I'm concerned with what William thinks. Right now, I hope he's thinking exactly what I'm thinking, and that is we are out of here and heading for his place, honey."

"I'll say," said Betty. "Go on, now." She laughed.

Christy got out of the line and headed for the men's room inside the dark and noisy club. As Christy entered the men's room, she encountered a gray-haired man from the wake zipping his pants while standing in a crouched position.

"Hey, Missy, either you ain't supposed to be in here, or I'm drunker than I thought."

"Neither one, Old Fool. Now vanish," Christy said in a deep voice.

"I must be drunk," said the old man as he stumbled out of the men's room.

Kenneth entered the club and sat at the bar while scanning the dark room in search of William. He spotted William with Nathan, then ordered a drink to help him build his nerves. He sipped his drink, still watching William's table, trying to monitor the moods. He knew he would have to choose the perfect moment to try and talk with William again. Experience had taught him that sometimes he had to be in the proper place to cuss William out in order to get his attention. Ken cared about his older cousin William and did not want the townspeople to have any unnecessary ammunition to hurt him. He decided to risk life and limb by telling William his news about Christy whether he wanted to hear it or not.

Just as Ken started to approach William's table, he saw Christy taking a seat next to William. Ken slowed in his tracks, then walked in another direction. He settled in the corner of the club and beckoned the waitress into the darkness. The waitress walked over to Ken and lowered her ear to his face. She then walked directly to William's table and leaned down and relayed a message to William.

"Who wants me?" William yelled over the music.

"The guy said he is an old friend who wants to surprise you. I'm simply giving you the message. So you coming or what?" the waitress asked.

"Yeah, shoot. Who in the world is playing with me? I will be right back, Baby," William whispered to Christy and kissed her on the neck.

William followed the waitress to the corner in the dark club, fussing all the way. He began yelling as he neared the table and recognized Ken smiling at him.

"Ken, Man, what you want disturbing me? Can't you see I'm taking care of business? You are worse than a little child or a bad penny that keeps turning up. Maybe you need to get yourself a woman so you can have some business to settle."

"Naw, William, this ain't no joke, Man. I hope you don't think I drove all the way up here to tease you. I thought about this, and I decided the right thing to do was to tell you the truth, because I sure would want somebody to tell me before I went too far."

"What you talking about, Ken? Go ahead and say it. We were getting ready to go anyway."

"You can't leave with her, William."

"Ken, go home, if that's all you have to say. I'm out of here."

"William, she ain't no woman. Man! She, I mean-"

"What! What you talking about, Ken? How come she ain't no woman?"

"Cause she is a man, William."

"You're a liar! Ken, I swear there must be something wrong with you."

"William, Mama swears Christy is a man."

"What? How does she know who's a man or a woman?"

"She knows, Man. My mother knew Christy and Darla in Chicago. Mother says Christy is most definitely a man. I would not lie to you, Buddy. My mother told me to be sure to find you and tell you before things got too out of hand. She does not want anybody to get hurt, Man."

William stood motionless, staring at Ken without uttering a sound.

"Say something William. I had to tell you, Man. Are you okay?"

"It's already too late, Ken."

"Oh no. Don't tell me y'all-"

"Naw, man. Not that, but everybody already saw me with that...What am I supposed to do?"

"They do not know about Christy. I ain't told nobody a thing. So you can tell whatever story you want to tell."

"Ken, I'm leaving without telling her anything, because if I go back to that table, I will hurt her. I don't play that mess."

"No, Man, we cannot have no trouble. That will get people to talking, and I know you do not want that. The best thing to do is to disappear, and I will tell Christy you had to leave. I will offer her a ride back to Miss Bessie's house. Christy won't suspect a thing, and that will be the end of that. She will be okay."

"Stop saying she or her. It is a man! Oh, God, it makes me sick to think about it," William shouted. How could I be so stupid?"

"Calm down, William. Turn and walk on out of here. I will head for the table as you head out of the door."

"But, Ken-"

"Go ahead, Man. Don't worry. I will handle this nice and quiet."

"Okay, Ken. Let me know how it goes. I will see you tomorrow, but please keep it to yourself, Man? Lord, if those guys on the job get wind of this, I will have to leave town. Don't tell, Ken."

"I won't, Man."

William sneaked out of the club as Ken walked back to the table and sat beside Christy. Nathan looked around the club as Ken explained to Christy.

"What is this?" Christy questioned in a roar. "How dare he leave without me?"

"An emergency came up," Ken lied.

"Emergency, my-"

"Christy, William asked me to give you a ride to Miss Bessie's. Is that okay?" asked Ken?

"What choice do I have? I do not know anybody in this ridiculous place. I don't really know you, except for today."

"I'm Ken, Ruth Ward's son."

"Ken, I don't know you. Where do you get off-?"

"I'm Ruth Ward's son."

"Ruth Ward, Ruth Ward, from where do I know that name?" Christy questioned.

"My mother lives in Chicago," Ken stated flatly while staring Christy in the eyes.

"Oh...that Ruth Ward." Christy's voice trailed off.

"Yes."

"I see! Well, Ken, I guess we might as well go."

"Yep, I'm afraid so."

Christy stood and extended her hand to Nathan and Betty.

"Nice meeting you guys. See you at the funeral."

"Same here, Christy. Sorry y'all got to leave so soon," Betty said as Nathan's eyes scanned the club for William.

When Christy and Ken reached the car, Christy turned to Ken and said, "I was going to tell him when the time was right."

"I don't know anything about that, Christy. I'm only here to take you home. Let us leave it at that, okay?"

As the crowd began to empty the little church at the end of the funeral, Christy walked over to William, who was hiding in his car. He had sat in the back of the church during the funeral. Once during the service, Christy caught a glimpse of William slumping in his seat in the back pew. Most of the church members stared at him and laughed every time he looked back at them. He had no idea who had told, but he suddenly felt everyone knew. He wondered how long it would be before they stopped looking at him and laughing. At some point or somewhere between the musical numbers and the family crying, William had eased out of the church.

Christy looked and headed straight for William's car. William sat upright in the car when he realized Christy saw him. He braced himself for a public confrontation. Most of the people were staring as Christy walked to William's car and tapped on the window. She leaned down and said, "I want to say good-bye to you and to let you know it could have been interesting."

"Oh, yeah. You would think that," he said, grumbling.

"Well, we will never know," Christy said, smiling. "Besides, everyone thinks we did anyway. Good luck convincing them that we didn't." She smiled before she turned and walked toward the family's limousine.

Introducing the book, **<u>MORE THAN IT SEEMS</u>**, the first book of a trilogy in the Jimmy Jurrell High School Easy Peezy Series. Join in the discussion with our high school book club members at:
authorenakevwe@gmail.com

Author's Marketing Page

Name pronounced: Lin dah Scott   Enak ev vey

Twitter: Linda Scott Enakevwe

Instagram: Enakevwe

Facebook: author linda scott enakevwe

Email address:

authorenakevwe@gmail.com